Hands Off My Stuff!

Written by Julie Sykes
Illustrated by Jess Mikhail

Published by Pearson Education Limited, Edinburgh Gate, Harlow, Essex, CM20 2JE.

www.pearsonschools.co.uk

Text © Julie Sykes 2013

Original illustrations © Pearson Education Limited 2013
Illustrated by Jess Mikhail, United Agents

The right of Julie Sykes to be identified as author of this work has been asserted by her in
accordance with the Copyright, Designs and Patents Act 1988.

First published 2013

17 16 15 14 13
10 9 8 7 6 5 4 3 2 1

British Library Cataloguing in Publication Data
A catalogue record for this book is available from the British Library

ISBN 978 0 435 14368 8

Printed and bound in the UK by Ashford Colour Press.

Acknowledgements
We would like to thank Bangor Central Integrated Primary School, Northern Ireland;
Bishop Henderson Church of England Primary School, Somerset; Bletchingdon Parochial
Church of England Primary School, Oxfordshire; Brookside Community Primary School,
Somerset; Bude Park Primary School, Hull; Carisbrooke Church of England Primary School,
Isle of Wight; Cheddington Combined School, Buckinghamshire; Dair House Independent
School, Buckinghamshire; Glebe Infant School, Gloucestershire; Henley Green Primary
School, Coventry; Lovelace Primary School, Surrey; Our Lady of Peace Junior School,
Slough; Tackley Church of England Primary School, Oxfordshire; and Twyford Church of
England School, Buckinghamshire for their invaluable help in the development and trialling
of the Bug Club resources.

Every effort has been made to contact copyright holders of material reproduced in this book.
Any omissions will be rectified in subsequent printings if notice is given to the publishers.

CONTENTS

CHAPTER 1
TARA ARRIVES

It's the first day of the school holidays and I should be happy but I'm not. I'm very unhappy because today my stepsister Tara is coming to stay for two nights. At least she has her own bedroom now. Last time she came to stay, our spare room was cluttered up with Alex's drums and she had to share with me which was a disaster! Alex is Tara's dad. He's also

stepdad to me, Lily Good, and my little brother Dan. Mum said that Dan and I have to be VERY nice to Tara because it's not easy when your dad is living away from you, but it's not easy for me either. That's why I'm writing a guide on how to be a good stepsister. It's full of GOOD advice to help me be nice to Tara.

While Alex was collecting Tara, Dan and I sat in the kitchen with Mum eating biscuits and thinking up ways to make her feel part of the family.

"We could go for a picnic," I suggested.

Mum's picnics are legendary. She makes sandwiches with cool fillings like chicken mayo, or tuna and sweetcorn. There are mini quiches, cold pizza, tiny tomatoes, carrot sticks, crisps and dip. There's always home-made cake, too.

"That's a great idea, Lily," said Mum. "Where shall we go?"

We were still deciding when Tara arrived. My stepsister travels like a celebrity, with a ton of bags. She acts like a celebrity too, expecting everyone to carry them for her. Tara plonked herself down at the kitchen table while Alex staggered in with all her stuff. Mum went to help him.

Tara winked at Dan. "Look at you!" she exclaimed. "You've grown taller."

"Have I?" said Dan, sticking out his chest.

"Definitely," said Tara, her gaze resting on me. "You're growing too, Lily. It must be all those biscuits."

I was about to make an unkind comment when I remembered being nice.

Instead I said, "We're going out tomorrow. We thought it would be fun to go for a picnic."

Tara shuddered.

"A picnic! You guys really know how to live it up."

"I know," said Dan happily, misunderstanding Tara's comment. "Mum makes the best picnics ever."

Tara rolled her eyes. You could tell she was wishing she was somewhere else.

"So where are we going for this amazing picnic?"

"The lake's good," said Dan. "It's got a man-made beach."

"I don't do man-made beaches," said Tara. "I only like woman-made ones."

Confusion spread across Dan's face. To stop Tara teasing him further, I said, "Or we could go to the Lookout. It's this huge tower in the woods."

"We could go to the castle," said Dan, bouncing on his chair.

"Not the castle!" I groaned. "It's mostly a ruin."

"The dungeons are still there," said Dan.

"I hate the dungeons. They're dark and spooky and full of spiders."

"What's dark and spidery?" asked Alex, coming into the room with Mum.

"Lily's bedroom," quipped Tara, "and some castle ruins Dan's been telling me about." A cunning look crossed her face. "It sounds brilliant."

"It's not that great. Once you've seen the dungeons, there's nothing much to do," I said.

"Lily, that's not true," said Mum. "There's a huge field for playing football."

TARA'S FAVOURITE...

NOT!

Right, because Tara was really up for a game of footie. But Tara was nodding enthusiastically as if football was her most favourite thing in the world.

"So can we go to the castle?" asked Dan.

Tara gave a long sigh.

"No, Dan. Lily doesn't want to."

"Lily doesn't mind," said Mum.

Lily doesn't mind. Wow! I swear I said that without even moving my lips.

Mum opened the tall cupboard and pulled out two tins of sweetcorn.

"You girls can help me get the picnic ready for tomorrow."

BUT I DO MIND

ZIP

"I'd love to but I have to unpack." Tara was already out of her seat and diving upstairs like a runner bean on legs.

"And I have to rearrange my socks."

A lame excuse, I know, but my brain had gone like mush and I couldn't think of anything else.

"Your socks can wait," said Mum, handing me a loaf of bread. "Now start buttering, young lady!"

SPEEDY BEAN

Ages later there was a mound of buttered bread higher than Everest. I'd also chopped enough carrots and cucumber to feed every mountaineer who'd ever climbed it. Exhausted, I went upstairs. Tara's door was half-open and I could see her sprawled on her bed, earphones in, listening to music on her new smartphone. Her bags were on the floor still unpacked. What a cheat!

While I'd been working like a slave, she'd been lying around like a princess. Maybe she needed help? Unpacking is like rocket science, right? It's complicated. So the sisterly thing would be to go and show her how it's done.

LILY'S GUIDE TO UNPACKING:

STEP 1: UNZIP BAG.
STEP 2: TIP BAG UPSIDE DOWN OVER TARA'S HEAD.

Trouble is, I think Mum would show me her two-step guide:

STEP 1: SEND LILY TO HER ROOM.

STEP 2: ONLY LET HER OUT WHEN SHE'S OLD ENOUGH TO LEAVE HOME.

Perhaps I'd give the unpacking a miss. Instead I went to my room and wrote in my Good Stepsister's Guide.

UNPACKING IS HARD WORK. ONLY OFFER TO HELP YOUR STEPSISTER UNPACK HER SUITCASE IF YOU HAVEN'T JUST WASHED UP.

CHAPTER 2
HIDE AND SEEK

The following morning everyone was up early except for Tara. It took Alex forever to coax her out of bed. I could have got her up immediately – only pouring cold water on her probably wouldn't have been very stepsisterly.

Getting Tara up was only half the problem. Dressing was the real challenge. Three changes of outfit later she still wasn't ready. She stomped out of her room clutching an enormous wash bag.

"There's no mirror," she complained.

"Use the one in the hall," said Alex.

Tara rolled her eyes but Alex was too busy helping Mum to pack up the picnic hamper to notice. I hoped they'd put enough in for tea as well because at this rate we were going to need it.

"Lily, go and put the picnic rugs in the car," said Alex, when he saw me hovering.

I decided to take my Good Stepsister's Guide as well. I had a strong feeling I was going to need it. Tara was blocking the hallway. She'd pinned her long wavy hair into sections and was combing out one strand at a time.

"Are you looking for head-lice?" I asked her, jokingly.

Good thing I'm not a plant because the look she gave me was withering.

LILY

"I'm brushing my hair."

"We're going on a picnic, not a film shoot," I said, just in case she'd misunderstood.

"Really? Your outfit's saying 'trip to the dump'."

PRINCESS TARA

Tara's laughter followed me out to the car. I glanced down at my clothes: t-shirt, jeans and trainers. It wasn't as special as her sparkly white top and tiny skirt. It was a lot more practical, though. I couldn't wait to see her cross the field to the castle in her NEW boots.

Sadly I didn't get to.

"You can't wear those," Alex said to Tara, when we were getting into the car. "Go and put your trainers on."

Tara argued but Alex insisted that she got changed. It only took another fifteen minutes!

"Let's play 'I Spy'," said Dan, when we were finally on our way.

"I'd rather listen to music on my phone," said Tara, putting her earphones in and closing her eyes.

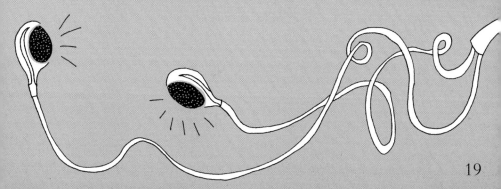

So much for a family day out! Tara didn't speak to anyone all the way there. When Alex parked in the castle car park, she watched while we unloaded the picnic, her head nodding in time to her music.

As we walked through the woods to the castle, Alex and Mum carried the picnic hamper and Dan and I carried the rugs. Tara carried her phone.

When we came out of the woods, Dan dumped his rug on the grass.

"Race you to the ruins," he shouted.

Throwing my rug on the ground, I ran after him. I could have easily overtaken him but he IS my little brother, so I didn't.

"Where's Tara?" asked Dan, when I finally caught up with him.

We both turned and saw Tara sitting on the rug, her head still nodding like one of those wobbling dogs people have in cars. It was tempting to leave her by herself but that wouldn't make me a good stepsister.

Swallowing back a sigh, I went to get her. Tara must have sensed me standing over her but she acted as though no one was there. I tapped her arm and was surprised with the force that she used to swat my hand away.

"Ooh sorry, Lily," she said, not sounding even a teensy bit sorry as she pulled out one of her ear plugs. "I thought you were a fly."

"Buzz, buzz," I answered. "Do you want to come and look at the castle?"

"What castle? All I can see is a big pile of stones."

"That's the castle," I said.

"In that case, I think I'll give it a miss," said Tara.

"We're going to eat now," said Mum brightly, waving Dan over to join us.

Mum set out the food and handed around plastic plates. It all looked so good I took a bit of everything.

"Are you going to eat all of that?" exclaimed Tara.

"No, I'm going to wear it," I retorted.

I bit into a cherry tomato. Unfortunately it exploded like a cannon, splurging pips and juice right down Tara's sparkly white top.

"Now *I'm* wearing it!" she exclaimed.

I had to bite the inside of my mouth so that I didn't laugh out loud. Mum leapt into action, dabbing at Tara's stained top with a tissue. Tara ranted on about how clumsy people like me shouldn't be allowed to eat dangerous food like tomatoes. I wanted to giggle. I was at bursting point from holding it all in. Quickly, I dug in the bag for my notebook and wrote down my latest piece of helpful advice.

CHERRY TOMATOES ARE **DANGEROUS**.

NEVER EAT THEM NEAR YOUR STEPSISTER WHEN SHE ISN'T WEARING RED CLOTHES OR SHE MIGHT END UP LOOKING LIKE ONE.

DANGER

Dan finished his lunch first and then asked Tara and me to play hide and seek with him.

"Okay," said Tara.

I didn't like the look on her face and I was even more suspicious when she made me count first.

"Close your eyes, then," she said bossily, as she and Dan prepared to hide.

I counted to a hundred, speeding up towards the end to yell, "Ready or not, I'm coming!"

97, 98... 99... 100!

Tara and Dan had chosen their hiding places well. There was no sign of either of them. Leaving Mum and Alex deep in conversation, I began my search. I started with the woods surrounding the field. There were lots of places to hide and I searched carefully. Tara and Dan weren't there so I ran over to the castle ruins.

The place had an empty feel to it. I looked behind the crumbling walls and piles of stone until there was only one place left to look. I stood at the top of the narrow stairs to the dungeons. Was I brave enough to enter them alone?

The staircase spiralled into the darkness. My heart tapped against my chest as if trying to get my attention.

"Don't do it," it said.

I didn't need much persuading. I'm such a coward when it comes to the dark. I'm an even bigger coward where there might be spiders involved too.

Leaning over the staircase, I yelled at the top of my voice, "I give up! Come out, wherever you are."

The darkness swallowed my words.

"You win!" I shouted more loudly, earning myself a wave from Mum.

There was no answer. But I knew they had to be down there. Where else could they be?

Reluctantly I walked halfway down the spiral stairs.

"Tara! Dan!" I yelled. "You can come out now. I give up!"

The silence was so loud it hurt. The noise of my heart thundering against my chest hurt more, though. Keeping one hand on the wall for balance, I continued to the bottom of the staircase.

"Tara, Dan?"

As I stepped into the dungeons something grabbed me. I tried to pull away but the grip on my arm tightened.

"Aaaargh!" I shrieked.

CHAPTER 3
THE WATER FIGHT

"Ouch! There's no need to bash me quite so hard," said Tara's voice in my ear.

"You!" I could barely get the words out.

"Well, duh!" said Tara. "Who else did you think it would be?"

Dan's shadowy face swam in front of me. He was doubled up with laughter.

"You screamed like a baby," he chortled.

Anger flooded through me. I turned and marched back upstairs. Tara and Dan followed, giggling together.

Out in the sunlight I turned to face them.

"Why didn't you answer when I called?"

"Did you call us?" Fake surprise was written all over Tara's face. She turned to Dan. "We didn't hear you. We were sharing music on my phone, one ear bud each, weren't we Dan?"

Dan mumbled something without looking at me.

Thanks, Dan. It's nice to know where your loyalties lie.

"Let's play again," he said. "I'll count this time."

I shook my head. I was too angry and hurt to speak.

"No, thanks," said Tara. "We've used the only decent hiding place there is. I want to go home now."

After one very long game of football between Alex and Dan, we finally packed up and went home.

ALEX LET DAN WIN.

"I'll sit in the middle," said Tara. "Then Dan and I can play Banana Bash together on my phone."

The look that passed between Mum and Alex almost had me reaching for a bucket to be sick in. They were thrilled that Tara was making an effort to be nice to Dan.

But what about me? Didn't I get to join in with a spot of banana bashing? Or was it obvious that it wasn't bananas I wanted to thump?

When we arrived home, Tara went to go upstairs. Mum stopped her.

"You girls can empty out the picnic hamper and wash everything up."

"Not me," said Tara, hopping round her. "I've got to practise some dance moves. I'm competing next week."

Mum blocked her way again.

"The hamper won't take long," said Mum pleasantly.

They stared at each other for a minute. A muscle twitched near Tara's jaw.

"Fine," she said at last. "I'll wash, but only if you have rubber gloves so I don't ruin my nails."

We unpacked the hamper in silence, Tara with her nose so turned up I was amazed she could breathe. We tipped all the dirty things into the sink. Tara filled it with water and half a bottle of washing-up liquid. Soon there were bubbles everywhere. You could tell she had never washed up before.

"This one's still dirty," I said, dropping a plate back into the water.

A dollop of bubbles flew up and landed on Tara's nose.

"Urrgh!" She wiped them away and then scooping up a handful of bubbles, flicked them at me.

Splat! They landed in the middle of my forehead and slid towards my eyes.

I giggled and plunged my hands into the washing-up water to flick some bubbles back. I didn't actually mean to throw a gallon of water with it. Tara gasped as the frothy warm water hit her in the face.

Time seemed to freeze. Now I was in for it. I'd probably be grounded and lose pocket money too. A weird sound erupted from Tara.

Laughter!

Faster than a thunderbolt, she scooped up some water with cupped hands and let me have it. Water splashed in my face and I snapped my mouth shut before I swallowed any. Giggling like idiots, we jostled each other at the sink in our efforts to drench each other.

"Stop!"

Mum's voice, sharp as broken glass, cut through our giggles.

"How could you? Look at the mess!"

It was pretty impressive. Bubbles slid down the walls and the floor was like a paddling pool. Tara's hair had all the appeal of rats' tails, but at least the stain on her T-shirt was beginning to fade. My curls stuck to my face in tight springy coils. Mum's eyes bulged like a tree frog's.

"I'm leaving this room and, when I come back, I expect to find everything back to normal. Is that clear?"

Tara's eyes met mine. She looked as though she'd swallowed a whole jar of marbles and was trying not to spit them out. I knew how she felt. Laughter was bubbling inside me like hot lava. We both nodded at Mum who thankfully left. We waited a nanosecond after the door had closed before we erupted. I was laughing so hard, I slipped on the wet floor. I landed on my bum and when I stood up, there was a huge patch as if I'd wet myself. Tara could hardly stand for laughing. It was ages before we calmed down enough to clear up the mess.

"That was so worth it," said Tara, pulling the rubber gloves off with a snap.

"Definitely."

NICE TREE FROG IMPRESSION MUM!

I followed her out of the kitchen. We parted at our bedroom doors. Tara opened her mouth as if she had something else to say, but nothing came out.

I waited a second then held up my hand. Wordlessly we high-fived! I was still grinning after I'd changed out of my damp clothes. I opened my notebook and flipped through it until I found my entry about tomatoes. Picking up my pen I added an extra tip:

IF YOU DO HAPPEN TO MESS UP YOUR STEPSISTER'S CLOTHES, MAKE SURE YOU HELP HER WASH THEM.

CHAPTER 4
BROKEN

I always get up early in the morning, even on a Sunday when most people lie in. This Sunday when I drew back my curtains, I was amazed to see Tara in the garden. I watched her for a bit. She was practising a dance routine. I always imagined that Tara dancing would be about as graceful as a stick insect on roller skates. She was really good at it, though. She made it seem easy and fun. Gathering all my courage, I decided to ask if she'd teach me a few dance steps. I grabbed a pair of shoes and opened my bedroom door. I wasn't the only early bird. Dan was just coming out of Tara's room. He didn't see me as he tiptoed across the landing to his own.

"Tara's in the garden," I called softly, so as not to disturb Mum and Alex.

Dan didn't hear me. The bedroom door closed. I didn't go after him. It would be nice to have some more time with Tara on my own. I was surprised to find Mum in the kitchen drinking from a mug of tea. What was it with my family today? Couldn't they sleep?

"You're up early," I said.

"That's Alex's fault," she yawned. "Last night he remembered he needed new guitar strings for the concert he's playing in next week so he got up early and went into town."

Just then the back door opened and Tara crashed through it.

"Need music ... getting my phone," she said, darting towards the stairs.

I hung around the kitchen waiting for her to return until an angry yell made me jump.

"My phone!"

Feet thundered down the stairs. Tara burst into the kitchen. She was crackling with anger. You could almost see fireworks fizzing in her eyes.

"It's broken!" she yelled, thrusting her phone at Mum.

Mum took it from her and examined the cracked screen.

"Oh dear," she said. "How on earth did that happen?"

"I. Don't. Know." Tara spat the words. "It wasn't broken when I went to bed."

"Did something fall on it in the night?" asked Mum.

"What – like an elephant?" Tara asked. "It was on my chest of drawers. How could anything fall on it?"

I edged towards the door.

"Where are you going off to, Lily?" Mum asked.

"To get Dan," I said, trying to act casually. "Maybe he knows something about it."

"Dan's not up yet."

"Yes, I am." Dan bounced in, smiling as if he didn't have a trouble in the world. "What's up?"

"This," said Tara, thrusting the broken phone at him.

Dan's face crumpled.

"Oh Tara!" he gasped. "I'm sorry. Did you drop it?"

Tara looked ready to throw the phone.

"No, I did not. Someone came in my room and broke it."

Fear flickered across Dan's face.

43

"Not me," he said firmly. "I definitely didn't do that."

I couldn't believe my ears. Were they hearing correctly? Maybe I should try shaking them the same way we shake Granny's television to get the sound to work properly.

"Are you sure?" Mum asked. "You didn't go into Tara's room and accidentally damage her phone?"

Dan's face was so tight, he looked like a wrung-out towel. Mutely, he shook his head.

"Well, someone has," said Tara, her voice rising, "and when I find out who did this, I'm going to …"

"Lily," said Mum, her voice cutting through Tara's. "Do you know anything about Tara's phone?"

All eyes turned to me. Tara clenched her fists. Her breath came in shallow snorts. I turned, slightly blocking her out as I raised my eyebrows at Dan. He had GUILTY stamped across his face. He shrugged and stared at his feet.

Good is our surname but Dan and I aren't angels. We often do things we shouldn't. But we're always honest. Or so I thought.

"Lily?" prompted Mum.

Dan looked ready to burst into tears. What a baby. Then suddenly I remembered: Dan IS a baby. He's four years younger than me. It's just that I forget sometimes because, as brothers go, he's generally all right. But today he was showing his young age by being too frightened to tell the truth.

"I did it," I gabbled on impulse. "I'm really sorry, Tara. It was an accident. I was going to tell you but I never got the chance and then I sort of panicked." I glanced at Dan in the hope that he might be prompted to own up. No chance. He was staring at me with a mixture of horror and relief.

"Oh, Lily," said Mum, her lips compressed in a tight line. "Why didn't you own up straight away?"

"I told you, I *panicked*," I said, locking eyes with Dan.

Mum lowered her voice in that annoying way adults have when there's bad news.

"I'm very disappointed in you."

Tara was so angry she was practically foaming at the mouth.

"How dare you touch my things?" she spat out. "You'll pay for this."

"She certainly will," said Mum, smoothly. "Lily will pay to have the phone repaired. She must also own up to her crime when Alex returns. She can ask him to drive her back to the shops to get the phone fixed."

Own up to my crime? She made it sound as though I'd committed a murder. Tara looked ready to commit murder too. Not that I blamed her. After all, I'd just confessed to sneaking into her room and messing with her stuff. It was hardly the act of a good stepsister.

CHAPTER 5
CONFESSION TIME

SHOPS ✗

HOME ✗

AUSTRALIA

Alex was ages returning from the shops. I hoped he'd got lost and made a small detour via Australia. I liked Alex a lot and I couldn't bear the thought of him being disappointed by my so-called *crime*. Tara shut herself in her room. Dan sat outside with his nose pressed to the door, begging her to come out. Tara ignored him so Dan gave up and started on me.

"Lily, go and be nice to Tara," he said.

"I'm always nice to Tara."

"But you have to be extra nice to her, now you've broken her phone."

My jaw dropped so fast it almost hit my feet. When I'd covered up for Dan, I hadn't meant for him to start believing the lie.

"Hang on," I spluttered. "Don't you have something you want to tell me?"

Dan frowned. He was concentrating so hard you could practically see the thoughts marching across his face. Finally he said, "No. I don't think so."

"I think you do," I insisted.

Dan thought about it some more and his face turned pink.

"It was a joke," he said eventually. "I thought you'd laugh."

"It's not funny, Dan."

"It was, sort of. The way you screamed." Dan's shoulders shook as he tried to hold back his giggles.

"I never screamed."

"Yes, you did. It was like you were in a horror movie. You jumped so high we thought you were flying."

"What are you talking about?"

"When Tara and I were hiding in the dungeons. We pretended we hadn't heard you call us so we could jump out on you. It was so funny." Dan trailed off when I didn't laugh with him.

"I'm not talking about yesterday. What about this morning?" I snapped. "What were you doing in Tara's room?"

Dan glared at me.

"Lily! Are you saying I broke the phone? That's bad when you know you did it."

"I didn't break it. I just said that to stop you from getting into trouble because I saw you come out of Tara's room."

Dan crossed his arms over his chest. "I was lending her my book on castles. Go and look if you don't believe me."

"But …" I said.

"You're horrible!" shouted Dan. "And you broke Tara's phone." He stomped to his room and shut the door.

Great! I get into trouble to save Dan and he ends up hating me. Life is so unfair. Our house was like a ghost town until Alex finally arrived home. Then, like little maggots in an apple, everyone wriggled out of their holes and gathered in the kitchen.

TARA

DAN

ME

MUM

Alex put a bag on the table.

"Confession time," he said, sitting down.

Heat flooded my face until I was so hot you could have cooked on me. How did he know I had a confession to make? Unless Mum had been busy on her mobile phone, or the jungle drums as Alex laughingly calls it.

Putting his hand into the bag, Alex drew out a slim white box and slid it over to Tara.

"This is for you. I'm sorry and I won't do it again."

Tara stared at the box suspiciously.

"What is it?" she asked.

"Well, I've wanted a smartphone for ages," said Alex. "So last night when you were asleep, I borrowed yours for a little try. Only I accidentally dropped it and smashed the screen." He pulled a sad face. "I'm sorry. This morning I got up early and bought you a new one. I hoped you wouldn't wake up until I got back. I'm going to get yours repaired and keep it for myself."

Tara looked like she was impersonating a goldfish. She opened her mouth and then closed it again.

"I don't understand," she said. "Lily broke my phone."

"I only said that because I thought Dan had done it," I said quietly.

Everyone stared at me. It was like being watched by a tank full of fish. They all had their mouths open.

"So you got yourself into trouble because you thought you were saving Dan?" asked Tara.

I nodded.

"Wow! I wish I had a sister like you!" She leapt up and hugged me tight.

"You do!" I said.

I'm not sure who was most surprised. As Tara pulled away from the hug, we both burst out laughing.

"Maybe this step-family thing isn't so bad after all," she said.

"It's not," I agreed. "Not if you follow the guide."

Tara looked confused.

"I'll show you later," I said. "It's not quite finished yet."

I would show her, but right now Mum had the frying pan out and my stomach was telling me that it had missed breakfast. One fried egg sandwich later, I went upstairs to add my final tip to my guide before showing it to Tara.

HUG YOUR STEPSISTER LOTS.
HUGS ARE A THOUSAND TIMES BETTER
THAN WORDS — UNLESS YOU'VE BROKEN
HER PHONE.